TUTANKH
IN MY OWN
Hieroglyphs

TUTANKHAMUN
IN MY OWN ~~WORDS~~
Hieroglyphs

WRITTEN AND ILLUSTRATED BY
LEENA PEKKALAINEN

The American University in Cairo Press

Cairo   New York

Leena Pekkalainen is a writer, blogger, and artist who studied Egyptology at Manchester University. Together with Mr. Mummific, who appeared on her sketchpad one day when she was taking a break from her studies, she writes about ancient Egypt on www.ancientegypt101.com. She is the author and illustrator of *How I Became a Mummy* (AUC Press, 2016), and *Mummies, Monsters, and the Ship of Millions* (AUC Press, 2017).

First published in 2018 by
The American University in Cairo Press
113 Sharia Kasr el Aini, Cairo, Egypt
420 Fifth Avenue, New York, NY 10018
www.aucpress.com

Exclusive distribution outside Egypt and North America by I.B.Tauris & Co Ltd., 6 Salem Road, London, W4 2BU

Dar el Kutub No. 13706/17
ISBN 978 977 416 866 6

Dar el Kutub Cataloging-in-Publication Data

Pekkalainen, Leena
    Tutankhamun: In My Own Hieroglyphs / Leena Pekkalainen.—Cairo: The American University in Cairo Press, 2018.
    p.   cm.
    ISBN 978 977 416 866 6
    1. Egypt—Antiquities
    932

1 2 3 4 5   22 21 20 19 18

Designed by Carolyn Gibson
Printed in China

CONTENTS

I

Akhetaten

Do you have any idea how bored you can get when you spend 3,300 years stuck in one place?

Bored, I tell you, very bored.

Of course, for my part I can say I was lucky enough to have plenty of interesting things to entertain me during that time, but still. Talking with the same statues and shabtis, and playing the same games inside my tomb all this time . . . well, it can drive you crazy. I ended up having long conversations with anyone and everyone in my tomb. Animals, goddesses, shabtis, beds (yes, beds!) . . . anything with a face, really (yes, my beds had faces). Sound sane to you? Thought not. . . .

Tomb, you ask? Shabtis and goddesses, you ask? Beds with faces, you ask?

Very well, let me start from the beginning. A very good place to start, as they say.

So, let me introduce myself: my name is Tutankhamun. What's yours?

(The polite thing is to tell me your name now.)

Nice to meet you.

Yes, I'm the same Tutankhamun whose name you've heard many times, I'm sure. I'm very glad that you've heard it, as every ancient Egyptian knows that as long as your name is spoken out loud you'll flourish in the afterlife. That's why we took such measures to write our names everywhere; on the walls of our tombs especially, and on the statues we placed in temples. Sometimes we wrote our names over those of other people. If you don't believe me, just ask any other pharaoh! I'm sure you've heard the name Ramesses before, yes? Thought so. I'm talking about Ramesses the Great. Number two, if you will, as there were eleven in all. Well, Ramesses the Second was especially eager to take over the monuments of his predecessors by having his own name written over theirs. My grandfather—the one you call Amenhotep the Third—was one whose magnificent statues

Ramesses stole a lot. And you call him Ramesses the Great! I call him lazy. I might even call him a thief, but I admit that was the way of things in our land—calling him a thief would force me to call just about every other pharaoh a thief, too!

The reason everyone had their names written, chiseled, and painted wherever possible was that with any luck people would see the name and say it out loud. The problem being, of course, that very few people in my time could read. That's why we paid the priests in the temples, so that they would keep on coming to our memorial temples and to our tombs to give us offerings and say our names out loud. That's why people so eagerly brought little statues with their names on them to temples: so they would not be forgotten. After all, the priests who moved about the temples were more likely to be able to read than other people.

I, for one, was certainly in danger of being completely forgotten. The kings that came after me tried to hide the fact that I had ever even been a king. Why? Well, they didn't like my father much. It wasn't fair to remove my name from my monuments, but what could I do—there I was, stuck in my tomb, and I couldn't even haunt them, no matter how much they deserved to be haunted. . . .

So, who was it who removed my name? Well, Horemheb, for starters. I was very disappointed with Horemheb. . . .

But as I said, it is best to start from the beginning.

I was born in the city of Akhetaten. You may not have heard of it before. My father Akhenaten had it built on the eastern shore of the great river you later began to call the Nile, in a place where no god had been worshiped before. That was very important to him. We Egyptians believed gods were everywhere, and that every town and city should have its own major god, together with the god's wife and child. Which meant there had to be a temple for them in the city.

But why did my father insist on building a city where no deity had ever had his (or her) temple, then? The reason was that he had ended up on rather bad terms with the priests of Amun in the capital, Thebes. Bad words were said on both sides, and in the end my father had had enough and started searching for a better place to live in—a place where there would be no priests of Amun.

As it happened, one morning my father was sailing on a ship on the Nile, minding the land's business, as is the duty of a king, and was up early to greet the rising sun. The sun rose above some cliffs, and together the cliffs and the sun looked a lot like the hieroglyph akhet, meaning 'the horizon.' See?

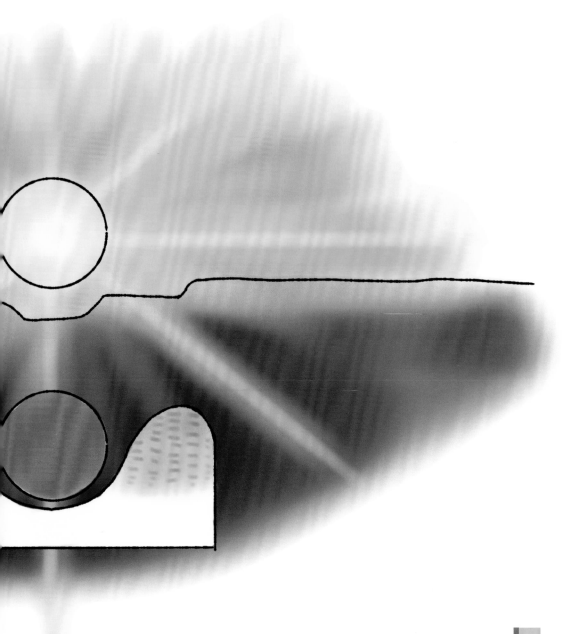

My father liked the sun a lot. As the god Aten—whom he liked most of all—was thought to be the sun's disk, he decided that he had found the perfect place for a new city. Akhet-Aten—the horizon of Aten. (Here's a picture of him and Aten, whose long rays end in hands.)

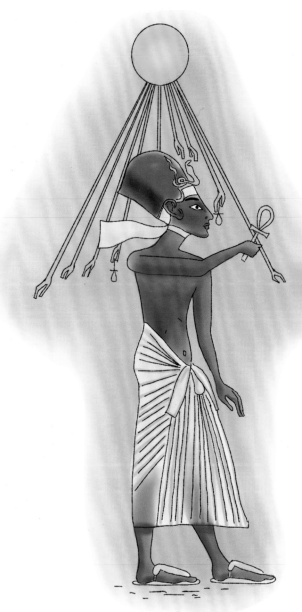

And so the city was built. My father was so peeved with the priesthood of the god Amun in Thebes that he preferred to stay in a tent at the site of the future city, and together with the architects, made a plan for it.

It was built very fast, in only a few years. I know people think that everything was made of stone in ancient Egypt, but no—it takes a lot of work to cut stone, so it was used only for great temples. Usually we built everything out of mud bricks. Even the king's palaces. Yes, you heard right: the pharaohs lived in mud-brick palaces.

And here in the new royal city of Akhetaten, the palaces and temples were also built out of mud bricks. Of course, the walls were plastered over and painted with beautiful pictures, so it all looked very pretty. And in fact some stone was used on doorways, lintels, and pillars—but stone was mostly reserved for the detail.

Since my father had decided that the court would move to this new city of Akhetaten, thousands of people had to leave the old capital of Thebes and follow him. A new city needed its workers. How else would the palaces have appeared in the middle of nowhere? How would the king and his family and court have eaten? Or worn clean clothing? Or have been entertained and beautified? Who would have taken care of the horses and the animals in the private zoo? Surely not the royal family—that was not the proper way of things. (We even had a goddess of the proper way of things: Ma'at. Here's a picture of her.)

And so the people who followed their king built the official buildings of the city, and also their own houses all around the city center. First-comers got the best plots, of course, and the rest squeezed their houses in where there was any room left. And so what was once a quiet plain between the sunrise and the river was now a buzzing city where the noise never seemed to stop.

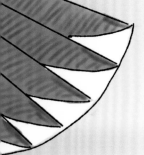

Life had already settled into its ways in the new city by the time I was born. And that's really where this story starts.

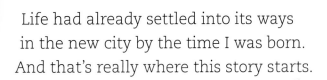

2 Fingers

I saw the sunlight for the first time not long before the Great Jubilation of All Nations in my father Akhenaten's twelfth year as king. My father wanted to show his beautiful new city to everyone, and invited thousands of people to his party. Even royalty from faraway lands took part—and those who weren't invited sent rather sour letters to my father, complaining about it. I was too young to understand or remember much about the Jubilation, but I was told later on that it was a great thing to behold. My father sat on a throne in front of all the guests, as did the Great Royal Wife, Nefertiti.

I had six sisters: Meritaten, Meketaten, Ankhesenpaaten, Neferneferuaten Tasherit, Neferneferure, and Setepenre. My sisters took great care of me. I almost think they thought of me as a new toy, probably because they didn't have much experience with brothers. They dressed me up, and rehearsed doing their eye make-up on me. Now, don't laugh— it was important to have beautifully painted eyes! I was a prince, after all, and royal children had their eyes painted. And the green malachite we used kept eye infections away.

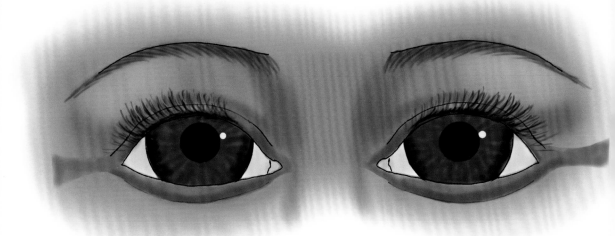

Of course, sometimes they got carried away, but I was too young to mind.

One of my fondest memories is of our private zoo. The people who came to my father's Jubilation brought exotic animals with them. And my sisters and I loved animals. We kept our favorites at the North Palace. That was the palace where Nefertiti lived. And us children, too, when we weren't in any of the other palaces. We liked the North Palace because of the beautiful paintings on the walls and floors, and because of the gardens and the animals.

We had ibexes, and gazelles, and antelopes there. And beautiful birds and a garden with a pool, which I fell into quite often. I didn't understand why everyone was in such a hurry to get me out of the water. I mean, the days were hot and the water was cool. What better combination?

"You are not a fish!" My nurse shook her finger at me after yet another episode involving cool water and servants chasing me in the pool to get me out. "Just look at your eye paint running!" My sisters glared at me, disappointed. They never put their heads underwater if they could avoid it. No wonder, considering how long they spent in front of the bronze mirrors painting their eyes.

I sulked—which usually worked to get me the things I wanted—but this time to no avail. I was most taken aback by the fact that even though I was a prince, no sulking or screaming would budge my nurse. She refused to let me into the pool, and everyone else seemed to support her opinion! They were in it together, a real conspiracy in my opinion. I tried to scream my anger, to see if that would help.

"Oh, shut up." My big sister Meritaten rolled her eyes to the sky. "A prince doesn't behave like that!"

I stuck my tongue out at her. She only lifted her eyebrow.

"He needs something else to think about," Meritaten then said to the other girls, who stood in a row and agreed with her as usual. "Something to keep him busy so we don't have to spend our days saving him from drowning. He doesn't know how to swim yet."

I was about to ask how I would ever learn to swim if I wasn't allowed to go into the water, but I shut up when I heard the question that Meketaten asked in response.

"Maybe horses?"

Now, that sounded like an idea—as the king, my father had the most magnificent horses. It was the custom of the king and the Great Royal Wife to race their horses from the North Palace to the great temples at the center of the city, using the broad Royal Road. The girls often went along in their chariots, but I was too small, they said, and would fall off. When I was older and taller, they said, that's when I could join them. But no matter how tall I tried to be, it seemed the day would never come when I'd race horses in a gilded chariot. They kept a record of my height against one of the pillars, and I tried to stand as tall as I could, but it seemed I grew very slowly.

But maybe now the day had come? I could almost hear the thunder of hooves, see the horses running with their long tails and their heads held high. Oh, surely there was nothing as beautiful as horses! It was a tradition in our family to be good at riding chariots. I intended to be the best—when I had the chance.

"Oh no, he's still way too young for horses!" the Great Royal Wife Nefertiti said, walking into the garden with Grandpa Ay.

I decided to continue sulking.

"Indeed, horses will have to wait for a while yet," Ay said. "But I think I have something to keep the boy occupied."

He clapped his hands and a servant walked over to us. On his shoulder was sitting . . . a small monkey!

"He is yours to keep," Grandpa Ay said.

"Oh, we want one, too!" The girls clapped their hands and rushed to take the monkey; they were always quick to snatch toys from me. But not this time!

"No! He's mine!" I stomped my foot on the ground.

"Girls, girls . . . you have enough pets as it is. The monkey is for Tutankhaten alone," Nerfertiti said, using my original name (I changed it to Tutankhamun later.) "Maybe it will keep him out of trouble."

Well, the monkey did no such thing—after all, that would have been asking for the impossible. Just think of it: a little boy and a monkey—how could such a pair possibly stay out of trouble?

I reached for the monkey, and he hopped on my shoulder and grabbed the lock of hair on the other side of my head. Like my sisters, I had one braid left to show that I was a child; the rest of my head was shaved bald. The monkey yanked the braid and pulled it to his mouth. I stood there, smiling broadly. The monkey was smiling, too. We were quite happy to be in each other's company.

"Look! They look just like each other!" Ankhesenpaaten giggled.

Me? Looking like the monkey? While I was still wondering if I should be angry at the comment or not, the monkey jumped from my shoulder to Ankhesenpaaten's and stole the grapes she was holding. The girls screamed, "A thief, a thief!" The monkey hopped back to my shoulder and started eating the grapes. He even gave me one.

I decided it wasn't so bad if they thought we resembled each other if the monkey managed to outwit my big sisters. And so, from that day on, my sisters called me the Little Monkey, while my light-fingered friend was known as Fingers.

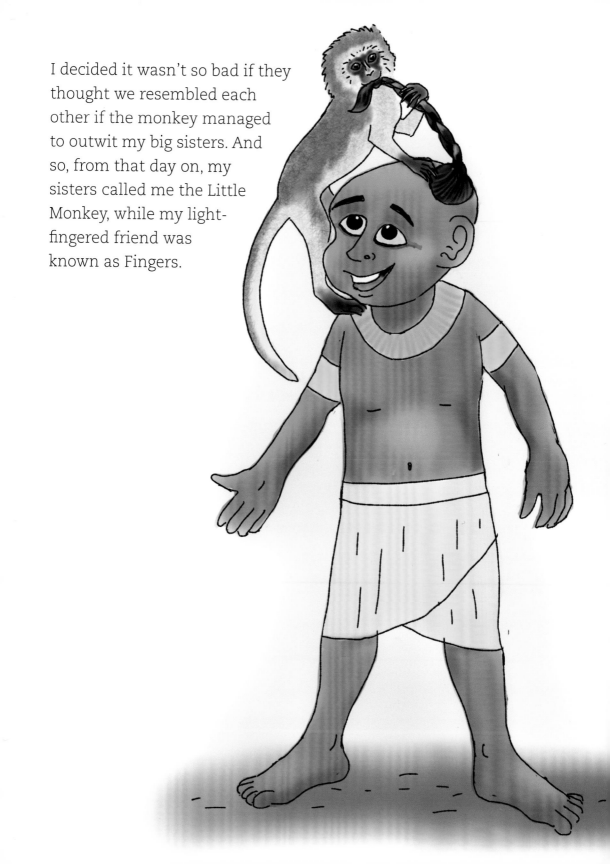

3 Meeting Horemheb

As a royal prince, I had to learn to read and write, and learn about what happened in the temples and the rest of the world. I wasn't all that interested in the rest of the world—everyone knew that Egypt was the best land, and anyone not born here was unfortunate. Still, the other lands existed and we traded with them, so I needed to learn about them, too.

And this meant going to school. It was called the kap, and was a place where the royal children and the children of high officials learned reading, writing, music, and mathematics. I hoped we would learn chariot racing and fighting as well, but much to my disappointment these things were not taught at school.

So, there I sat on the floor with the other children, including my sisters—no, we didn't have chairs; chairs were rare, so everyone usually sat on the floor. We sat cross-legged, stretching our kilts so that they were tight and could be used as tables, and resting gessoed wooden boards on this taut surface. And then we took our reed pens and inks, and copied old texts that were said to hold wisdom onto those gessoed boards. We learned that the only proper job was that of scribe (I thought it was to be king, but I soon learned that you weren't supposed to interrupt or disagree with the teacher, so after a few tries I said nothing). A scribe had a comfortable life, and enjoyed material wealth and the fruits of wisdom. All other professions apparently left people dead tired at the end of the day.

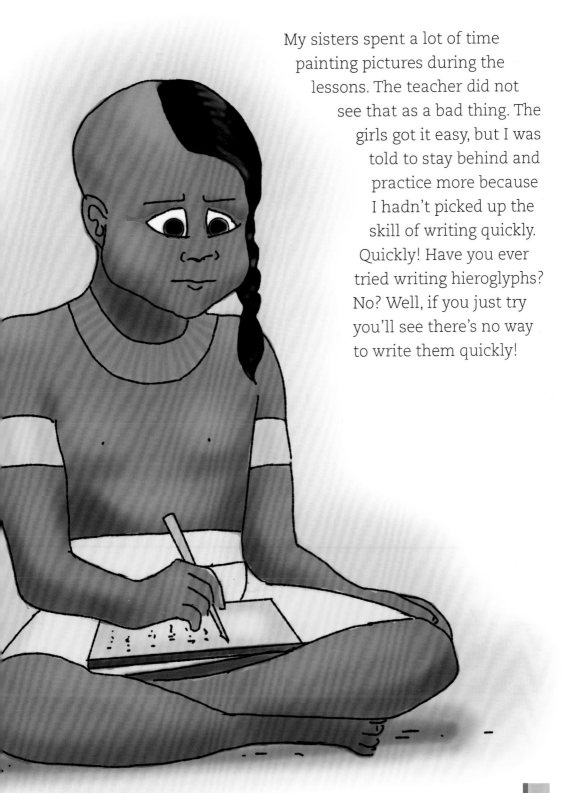

My sisters spent a lot of time painting pictures during the lessons. The teacher did not see that as a bad thing. The girls got it easy, but I was told to stay behind and practice more because I hadn't picked up the skill of writing quickly. Quickly! Have you ever tried writing hieroglyphs? No? Well, if you just try you'll see there's no way to write them quickly!

I wasn't very interested in reading and writing back then, but I tell you it would have been great to have something to read later in my tomb—anything, really. I often remembered those childhood days in the kap—whenever I looked at the palette of my sister Meritaten

that someone had placed in my tomb, I longed to be back there. If only they had placed those same writings we'd once copied inside my tomb, too. Like I said, death gets boring after a few hundred years in a tomb, so I wouldn't have minded a private library!

But did I enjoy being a child of the kap while it lasted? Oh my gods, no. I wanted to go out with Fingers, to race horses, to swim, to go see the animals. Anything but sit still, which was the most boring thing. I felt pity for my father, who had to tolerate sitting still for long hours while officials, petitioners, and people of all kinds asked him for things. Everyone had to bow deeply in front of him—some even lay flat on their stomachs! That was the only fun thing, in my opinion, about being a king: watching people bow and grovel on the floor. I was sometimes allowed to attend, but after Fingers stole the sandal of a foreign nobleman and I chased him around the hall, out the door, and into the gardens while trying to get it back, it was decided that it might be best if I didn't attend these official events too often. . . .

Fingers' thieving helped sometimes, though. Once, he stole the stick that the teacher used to tap out rhythms for our reading lessons (and occasionally to tap our backsides as well when we didn't concentrate). I kept quiet when I saw Fingers running off with the stick when the teacher dozed off. Others saw it, too, but they never said a word. Instead we all just tiptoed away and left the teacher snoring. The next day, we paid for it: no one was to leave the class until

everyone had copied the chosen text perfectly. As I tried for the fifth time, I sure felt the eyes of everyone else on me. They had managed to write flawlessly way before me. Even Fingers was sulking by the time I finished.

But then, after endless hours at the kap, the great day finally came: Grandpa Ay came to visit us. We—some of my sisters and I—were at the palace at the center of the city, near the sun temples. We had a day off kap, as our teacher was needed elsewhere—he was a scribe, after all, and the king's court had plenty of work for scribes. As one of those people who could speak and write foreign languages, he

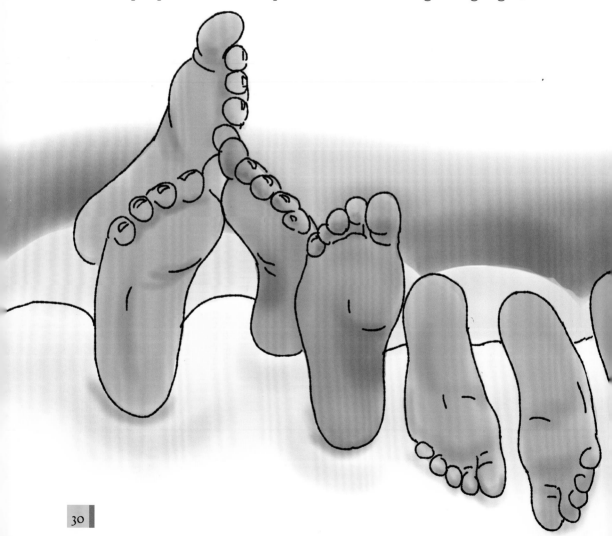

was asked to come and write a reply to a letter that a foreign king had sent to my father. Asking for gold, no doubt; these foreign kings were convinced we had gold lying about like sand, and were most offended when my father did not send them cartloads of it.

So there we were, doing nothing, when Ay marched in. He was not alone—I could see a young man standing behind him.

"Tutankhaten," Ay said, "I have come to introduce to you the man who will teach you all about horses and fighting. Meet Horemheb."

I was on my feet in an instant, almost embarrassed that this young man, Horemheb, had seen me lying on pillows. He would think me lazy! Well, I was lazy, but there's this thing called first impressions. I didn't want his first impression of me to be me lying on the floor on a hill of pillows with Fingers snoring next to me!

Horemheb walked closer and bowed deeply. He stayed in that position so long that Fingers went to him and tried to figure out what he was staring at on the ground—maybe a juicy insect? Ay pointed at Horemheb, and then at me, and coughed.

"Oh . . . right. Rise, Horemheb," I said, trying to sound royal.

He did, with a slightly flushed face. No wonder, having been head down for so long.

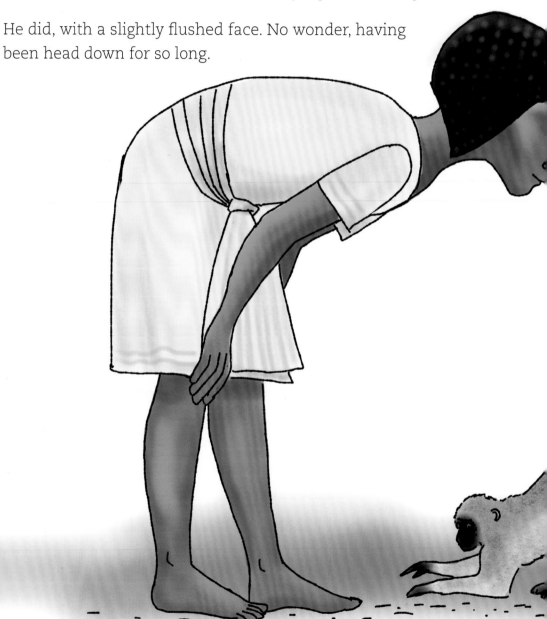

"I'm glad to meet you," I hurried to add. "I've wanted to race horses for so long!"

"I am honored to be chosen to teach a royal prince," Horemheb said. "Before this, I had the honor of training the horses of the mother of the king, Tiye—life, prosperity, and health to her."

My Grandma Tiye did indeed love her horses, as did my whole family. When my Grandpa Amenhotep was alive, they had hundreds of horses and loved to watch them race. (Here's a portrait of Grandma Tiye.)

Now, Horemheb fell quiet while Ay did all the talking.

"Horemheb has been instructed to teach you all about horses, racing, and fighting. He has been told not to be polite while teaching you. If you are to learn fighting skills, you must forget all about your position, and politeness. No one is polite on the battlefield."

"Of course!" I was more than happy to agree. After all, there had been no wars since . . . well, I didn't know. Many of my forefathers had been great warriors, but Grandpa Amenhotep had ruled over a time of peace. So I didn't really believe I'd ever end up on a battlefield. And actually I found the thought rather boring—instead I wanted to be a hero who captured whole cities and scared off whole armies single-handed. "When shall we start?"

"Tomorrow morning, two horses will be brought to you. You will start then. Oh, will you get lost!"

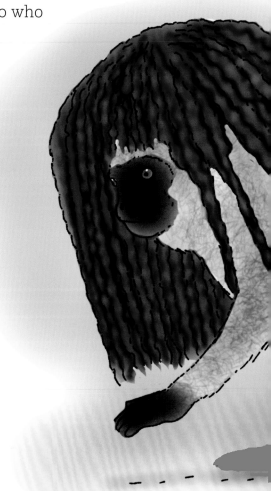

Horemheb glanced at Grandpa Ay, worried that he'd done something wrong. But it was just Fingers, who was in the process of trying to climb up Ay's kilt, managing to ruin his dignity. My sisters giggled at the sight.

"What about the kap?" I wanted to know.

"You have learned to read and write. You will continue to practice, but you don't need to spend every day in the kap any longer. These are the orders of your father, the king," Ay said, lifting Fingers off the ground and giving him to me. Fingers managed to catch hold of Grandpa Ay's wig in the process, causing my sisters to laugh out loud.

"If that is my father's wish," I said meekly, but it took all my self-discipline not to jump up and down and yell with joy. No more school!

I'm sure you understand.

4 Hoof and Tooth

And so, the next morning I marched to the stables to meet Horemheb. Perhaps today we would gallop down the Royal Road, waving to the cheering crowds.

Ha! No such luck.

It began in a promising way. Horemheb appeared in the stable yard, leading two beautiful horses—a bay one and a white one.
A white horse! They were rare. Everyone would envy me now!

"This is Hoof," Horemheb said, nodding toward the white horse. He didn't even greet me, which in my opinion showed bad manners. I had grown quite accustomed to the flowery language of the people of the court and their attempts to please me in case I would be the next king and would reward them later for showing respect to me. It was the way of things, and I had learned to expect such behavior from everyone.

But I was in a good mood, so I forgave him. Soon I'd be racing down the Royal Road like the wind!

"And this is Tooth." Horemheb nodded toward the bay horse.

"Hoof and Tooth?" I wasn't quite certain I had heard the names right. Surely royal horses should have names such as 'Beloved of Aten' or 'Aten Entrusts Him with Victory.' That was the way the king's horses were named according to tradition. But Hoof and Tooth? Who in their right minds would give horses such names?

"There's reason for the names. You'll learn it soon enough," Horemheb said, as if reading my thoughts. "Here, take Hoof's rope."

I approached Hoof and extended my arm, expecting the horse to come to me. After all, I was a prince and what I wanted was done. But the horse had not been taught good manners, either, for it did not budge. Horemheb threw me the rope, and I managed to grab it. The instant Horemheb let go of the rope, Hoof jumped to his hind legs and yanked himself free. I fell on my behind on the ground in a most undignified manner. Fingers, who had been sitting on my shoulder, shrieked, jumped down, and ran off.

"Lesson number one. Don't let your horse run free. When you hold the rope, hold it. Don't let go."

I watched Hoof running toward the stables.

"Well, what are you waiting for?" I asked Horemheb, who just kept standing there, holding Tooth.

"I'm waiting for you to go and get him back," he said.

"Me? But I'm a prince! Servants do all the fetching for me!" I was insulted.

"Not here, they don't. If you're to work with horses, you must know them. You must handle them so that you earn their respect. And that means teaching them that you're the boss; you say what can be done and what can't. That may save your life in battle. So go get Hoof. I'll wait here."

He really wasn't going to get the horse back! I opened my mouth to protest, but then remembered what Grandpa Ay had said. Horemheb was not going to be polite to me. If I wanted to learn to handle horses, Horemheb was the one I should stay on good terms with. And I really wanted to learn to race chariots.

So I sighed and walked toward the stables, mumbling under my breath. Hoof stood there waiting, and his ears flattened to his neck when I approached. He turned his rear toward me and lifted his hind leg. I suddenly understood why he was named Hoof. I concluded that Tooth was also called Tooth for a reason.

The morning hours passed while I chased Hoof around the stable yard. Much to my dismay, I heard the stable boys snickering as I ran around, all dusty, trying to corner the horse. Horemheb watched me for some time. When it became obvious that I wasn't ever going to catch Hoof, he finally approached me and gave me Tooth's rope.

"Better take hold of the rope quite near his head," he said, and I did just that. Tooth clacked his teeth and tried to bite me, but this time I wasn't going to let the horse go. We stared at each other gloomily.

When Hoof saw Horemheb approaching, he simply turned and walked right to him. Now the stable boys really did laugh, and I felt my cheeks burning red.

"Now, this is respect," Horemheb said. "When you earn the horse's respect, you won't have problems catching him."

I tried not to show how peeved I was, but didn't quite manage it.

"Very well, that's enough for today. Now we'll take the horses to their stable and feed and water them."

"I'm a prince, I don't . . . ," I began, but Horemheb interrupted me.

"Here you do. Remember, you must learn to know your horses. And there are advantages if the horse realizes you're the one who feeds him."

So I led Tooth to his stall and tied his rope so he couldn't run away, avoiding his teeth while I did so. Only when I brought the horses their food did their ears go forward, and they seemed to like me for a brief moment.

I was very disappointed in the way the horses had behaved. They should have behaved well, instead of running away from me or trying to kick me or bite me. Such disrespect for a royal prince! I was almost ready to give up on horses altogether at that point.

"One end kicks and the other bites . . . ," I mumbled to myself. Horemheb seemed to pay no attention to me.

But things got easier when I had bathed and was with my sisters again. They looked at me with more respect than before, and soon I had explained to them how I had my own pair of chariot horses now, and I was well on the way to becoming the best charioteer in the city. Their admiring comments made me decide to go back to the stables again.

I paid no attention to Grandpa Ay, who seemed to find my story of my own excellence somewhat funny.

Temple

Of course, I did actually have to try to ride my horses.

"Ride them? Sure, you can try," Horemheb said. "But princes don't ride horses. They drive chariots. Sitting astride a horse makes you look unroyal, and it isn't easy."

Still, I wanted to try. But after a few experiences of flying through the air, I decided that Horemheb was right. It was quite undignified to ride horses.

"Does anyone ride?" I asked, dusting myself off and counting my bruises while Tooth observed me from a distance, looking rather pleased with himself. Meanwhile, Fingers hopped on Hoof's back, and the ungrateful horse didn't mind him at all. Maybe it had something to do with the monkey's habit of sharing the spoils of his thieving sprees in the kitchens. The horses seemed to like fruit a lot.

"Yes, some people ride. But not us. And besides, no one's ever ridden Hoof or Tooth. It's clear they don't like it."

It seemed that these horses weren't meant for riding. By people, at least.

I finally got to ride my chariot to the great temple in the city early one morning not long after. Actually, Horemheb was at the reins, but I got to stand next to him. My chariot wasn't gilded and the horses weren't dressed up in colorful harnesses like the king's horses, but I didn't mind.

I tried to look nonchalant and hoped that as many of my schoolmates as possible would see me. Fingers sat on my shoulder, shrieking with joy, and I heard people shouting something about the Little Monkey. I felt a bit uneasy—had the pet name my sisters had given me become common knowledge? I hoped not. Being called a little monkey does diminish your prestige somewhat.

But what a wonderful experience the chariot ride was! Hoof and Tooth galloped with their heads held high, and a cloud of dust followed in our wake. The horses were breathing heavily as we arrived at the temple in the middle of the Avenue of Sphinxes.

"Are they having trouble breathing?" I asked.

"No, that's the way horses are supposed to breathe," Horemheb said, stepping down from the chariot.

I followed and patted the sweaty horses.

"Doesn't the collar choke them?" I asked, looking at how the horses' collars were attached to the pole that in turn was attached to the underside of the chariot. The horses pulled the chariot with their necks!

"That has to be there—how else could they draw a chariot?"
Horemheb asked. "But come, you're expected."

With Fingers balancing on my shoulder, we walked to the gates
of the great Aten Temple. The first pylon was arrayed with tall
flagpoles, which towered over it, and bright red flags snaked in the

wind. I stared at the flagpoles, not understanding how any tree could be so tall.

"Are those the trunks from real trees?" I asked.

"Yes, they are. Cedars of Lebanon are huge," Horemheb said. "Maybe one day I'll get to see them. . . . One day, I want to lead our troops to conquer foreign lands."

He gazed dreamily at the red flags above us.

"I might as well pop to see the trees while I'm at it," he added. "But you're expected, you must go inside now."

"Aren't you going to come?" I asked.

"No, not my place," Horemheb said, and turned back toward the horses.

I saw Grandpa Ay approaching from between the pylons of the temple. Behind them, I saw other pylons, painted with bright colors, showing the king and the Great Royal Wife receiving the blessing rays of Aten.

"Quickly now, we're about to start!" he said. "And keep Fingers near you. We can't have him running around free."

"Why not?" I asked, as we walked inside the great temple. "Oh, wow!"

Now I understood why. The huge open yard was filled with little offering tables. And each table was piled high with delicious food. I saw priests carrying even more food to the raised tables: bread, fowl, meat, fruit, and vegetables.

"Who gets to eat all that?" I asked.

Fingers seemed to know the answer. He was off my shoulder in an instant.

"Shoo!" A priest ran toward him, waving his hands. Then he saw us, stopped, and bowed low. Fingers took the opportunity to hop over his back to an offering table to steal fruit. Then he sat there, munching his spoils. This seemed to annoy the priest in question mightily. In fact, I'm certain I heard him using rather unpriestly terminology under his breath to describe my monkey.

"Monkey! Get off!" Grandpa Ay shouted at Fingers. "And you, get back to your work," he said to the priest, who straightened, flailing his hands to shoo Fingers away. Finally, he managed to drive the monkey to the ground and hurried off. "And you, hold Fingers so he can't escape again, and follow me!" Ay then said to me.

I grabbed Fingers, who was happily eating his way through a handful of dates. I was wise enough not to try to take them away from him—his screaming would have brought the guards in for sure.

It has to be said that Fingers did have some good manners, though; he offered me a date.

Grandpa Ay explained that the king and the Great Royal Wife were here to worship the rising sun, and all this food was for Aten.

"Really? The sun's going to eat all of this?" I asked him.

"Yes, this is all for Aten," he nodded.

I stared hard at the huge amount of food and waited for the sun to grab a goose leg at least, but none of the food disappeared, no matter what my father chanted.

"Maybe the sun isn't hungry," I said. "Can we go now?"

Grandpa Ay sighed and turned to leave. I quickly stole a pomegranate from one of the offering tables and followed him, hiding the fruit behind my back.

"Time for you to go to the kap again," he said. "In time, you will understand why all this is necessary."

Well, truth be told, I never really did. The sun didn't eat the food we offered it, but I noticed that many of the priests working at the temple looked rather chubby. But the general idea seemed to be that all this food was given to Aten so that he would keep on shining his bright light upon us and balance would prevail. Anyway, if the sun wanted to eat so much, who was I to argue?

I was more interested in my horses, no matter how badly they behaved.

6 Pharaoh

I was still quite a young boy when my father died and was given a splendid burial. I was too young to rule, though. I had never been interested in who was going to rule after him, because like every child I thought my father would live forever. Children don't think much about such matters.

Others did their best to govern the country after my father, but then the day came when I was the only eligible male left of my family line.

"Me? A king?" I asked Grandpa Ay as he stood in front of me, his face all lined with worry. So many had died in my family, and life was not fun any more.

"You. You are nine years old now, so we can crown you. We need a king to keep the country united. You will be crowned king, and I will help you to rule in every way I can."

Truth be told, I didn't want to be king. I wanted to race my horses and learn how to fight and shoot arrows from a moving chariot. But now even Horemheb started talking respectfully to me. Everything was upside-down.

It seemed I had no say in the matter, and so one day I was crowned king. Gosh, that double

crown was heavy! As for performing all the elements of the coronation . . . Grandpa Ay had to whisper to me all the time where I should walk, and when I should stop, and what I should say, and to whom. None of it made any sense to me. I just couldn't wait to get back to my horses.

But it seemed that after my coronation I was constantly surrounded by officials and people who wanted to please me and advise me. The members of the court who had taken the time to talk to me politely in the past now expected me to take them into my favor in return. But I did my best to get rid of them, and let Grandpa Ay decide who got positions in court.

For two years, I kept on living in Akhetaten. But the city wasn't the same any more, and people were beginning to move back to Thebes. So I had to do the same. I settled in my grandfather's old palace, which was quickly repaired for me and my court to use. But soon even that wasn't enough.

One day, I was a sitting with a sculptor who was preparing a portrait of me—or rather my head rising from a lotus flower as a symbol of new creation— when Grandpa Ay came to visit.

"You have to move to Inbu-Hedj," he said. "That is the ancient capital of our land, and you should move there and return the country to its old ways."

"What ways?" I asked.

"Well . . . your father did not tolerate gods other than Aten. And closing the temples of all the other gods and hacking their names from the temple walls caused much dissatisfaction. Priests were without work, and people had to move away from their old homes. . . ."

"Why?"

"Well, why do you think? They had to move to Akhetaten, of course." Grandpa Ay shook his head. "And now people

want their old lives back. You need to give permission for them to worship other gods again."

"By all means," I said, "if that makes them happy."

"There are so many dissatisfied people that we need to make a spectacle of returning to the old ways. And that's not all—you need to change your name."

Now, that was a bit much.

"What? I like my name!"

"You may like it, but others don't. Just a little change. You will go from Tutankhaten to Tutankhamun. That should make the priests of Amun happy."

My original name had meant 'the Living Image of Aten.' Now I would be 'the Living Image of Amun.' It seemed I had no say in the matter, and so my name was changed and I sailed to Inbu-Hedj (or Memphis, as you call it).

Years passed, and I got used to my new name. Fingers moved with me and spent happy times thieving from the palace kitchens, but even he got old, and one sad day, he passed away. I had him mummified and buried, hoping to see him again after I had died and had been properly mummified, too, so I could enter the afterlife.

Grandpa Ay did his best to make me interested in politics. Horemheb became an officer of the army, and I soon noticed that he and Grandpa Ay weren't on good terms with each other any more.

Horemheb was often away with the army. "I have to keep the borders of the land safe," I heard him say to another official when he visited my court. "The boy's father made no effort to protect this land. The army was in total disarray! I intend to put things right and make sure Kemet will be great again." ('Kemet' was the name we called our country—the name 'Egypt' was a later invention.)

When I relayed this to Grandpa Ay, he didn't say anything, but I could see he wasn't happy. I couldn't understand why; wasn't it a good thing that Horemheb wanted to protect the land?

It was only later that I understood what it was all about. Horemheb wanted to be king. And after I died, I learned that he did indeed become the king of Kemet.

He wouldn't have been able to do so if I had lived.

I should have lived a long life, but, as it happened, I died rather young.

I was nineteen years of age, and was walking in the palace garden with my wife Ankhesenamun when I got the idea to go drive my chariot. I had a new pair of fast horses I wanted to try out.

"Are you sure you need to go just now?" Ankhesenamun asked. "They're quite new horses, and you aren't used to them yet. I was thinking we could sit in the garden by the pool, and enjoy the cool wind."

"I want to do it now. I'm bored."

My wife sighed and kissed me on the cheek.

"Very well, if you wish. Come back safely!" she said.

Which, of course, I never did.

The next thing I knew, I was dead.

7 Painters

I'm still not sure what exactly happened. I just came to my senses standing in the middle of what was obviously a tomb.

Now, I didn't understand at first that it was my tomb. I had the most curious feeling that I'd forgotten something important. I remembered cheering my new horses on, very happy at their speed. I was being followed by other chariots manned by my closest friends. And then . . . the next thing I knew was that I was standing inside a small tomb, watching painters depict a scene on the wall. There was a figure of a pharaoh performing the Opening of the Mouth ritual on a dead person, who also appeared to be a pharaoh. If you haven't heard of this ritual before, it was only performed on someone who was dead and had been mummified. The idea was to awaken the senses of the dead person so that they could live again—to see, to hear, to smell, to speak. There were special tools used in this ritual, and in the painting the pharaoh was holding one of them in front of the dead person's face.

"Hmm, I wonder whose tomb this is . . . ," I said out loud, but no one paid any attention to me. This was strange. As a pharaoh, I was used to the fact that whenever I spoke, or even appeared anywhere, everyone would bow deeply in front of me. But these painters just kept on painting.

"Hurry up! We don't have any time to spare!" one of the men said. "The seventy days are almost up!"

Seventy days? I knew that that was the time it took to mummify a person. But what had that to do with them preparing this tomb? Tombs were always built well in advance so that you'd have one ready by the time you died.

"Just how many spots does a leopard have . . . ?" the artist in front of me sighed, painting little dots meticulously.

I looked more closely at the painting, letting the men get on with their work. I would comment on their impolite manners later. I mean, really, they behaved as if I wasn't there at all.

But back to the painting. The law dictated that the Opening of the Mouth ritual was performed by the dead person's heir. Without performing it, he wouldn't inherit a thing. And when it came to kings, it was the most important sign of who was going to inherit the crown. So, whoever was doing this Opening of the Mouth was declaring that he was the next pharaoh. And after the rites were done, no one could challenge that. It was the way of things.

"Why such a hurry?" a young painter wanted to know.

"This has to be done before Horemheb comes back!" the oldest of the painters said.

"Why?"

"So that Ay can perform all the rites before Horemheb tries to steal the crown!" the old man whispered, looking over his shoulder. His eyes looked straight at me, but he paid no attention to me. "But keep that to yourself. It's not safe for the likes of us to discuss these matters. Those in power can be dangerous!"

Ay? Horemheb? What on earth were these men talking about? I spun around to look at the other wall, which they had already painted. There was a pharaoh in a white kilt, a white headdress, and white sandals. The god of the underworld, Anubis, was standing behind him, and the goddess Hathor was offering a little ankh-sign to the nostrils of the king—the Breath of Life. That was a scene where the dead king was welcomed to the afterlife. . . .

The painters were talking about Ay and Horemheb as potential inheritors. That could only mean one thing: that the dead pharaoh was . . . me! After all, I had no children to pass my crown on to. But for gods' sakes, I felt quite alive!

I looked down at myself. I was still wearing the same clothes and sandals that I'd had on when I'd been racing my chariot. So the dead person couldn't be me—they would have taken off my clothes to mummify me, surely! I reached out with my hand and tried to touch the freshly painted wall. And that's when I understood that it had to be true. I could see through my arm, and my fingers did not pick up the wet paint. Also, the painter paid no attention to my hand poking at the surface in front of his face.

I don't know how you would have reacted, but the shock of realizing I was dead was such that I fainted.

Ba-Bird

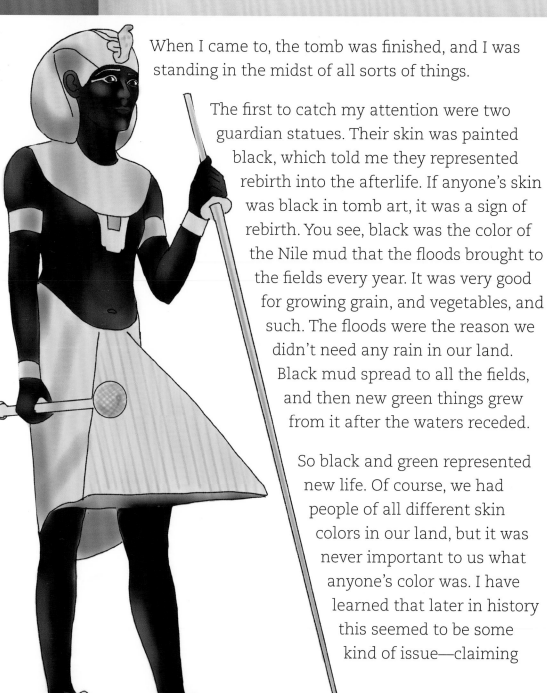

When I came to, the tomb was finished, and I was standing in the midst of all sorts of things.

The first to catch my attention were two guardian statues. Their skin was painted black, which told me they represented rebirth into the afterlife. If anyone's skin was black in tomb art, it was a sign of rebirth. You see, black was the color of the Nile mud that the floods brought to the fields every year. It was very good for growing grain, and vegetables, and such. The floods were the reason we didn't need any rain in our land. Black mud spread to all the fields, and then new green things grew from it after the waters receded.

So black and green represented new life. Of course, we had people of all different skin colors in our land, but it was never important to us what anyone's color was. I have learned that later in history this seemed to be some kind of issue—claiming that one person's skin color was better than another's—but we Egyptians would never have understood this. We preferred to judge people by what kind of people they were: what they had achieved, how they talked and treated others. (If you look at a skeleton, can you tell the person's skin color? Exactly. You can't.)

But back to my tomb. There I was, looking at the two statues. They were standing facing each other, sideways to me. On my left were three large animal-shaped beds. I turned around and saw chariots—dismantled chariots. I recognized the one I had been driving just before my . . . death.

I looked down again at my ghostly body. Yes, all the limbs were there. I saw just my ordinary self, no mummy wrappings or anything.

I whirled around. Where was my coffin? Was I stuck in one small room? With this much stuff? I could barely move in here!

"You might try walking through the walls," a voice said.

"Who? What? Who spoke?" I said out loud, and tried to see who was with me in my tomb.

"I did," the voice said.

I still couldn't see anyone.

"Be more specific!" I said.

A flutter of wings. A bird? Inside the tomb? I looked around, but saw no one. And anyway, how exactly was I supposed to see a thing? There were no openings in the walls, no torches or oil lamps, either. This had to be a skill dead people had to learn.

Someone yawned. My eyes caught movement on top of one the beds . . . the middle one, the one formed like a cow. Then two wings stretched upward, followed by another yawn. The bird got up and walked to the edge of the bed. Only it wasn't quite a bird. I mean, it had the body of a bird, but a human head. My head, to be exact!

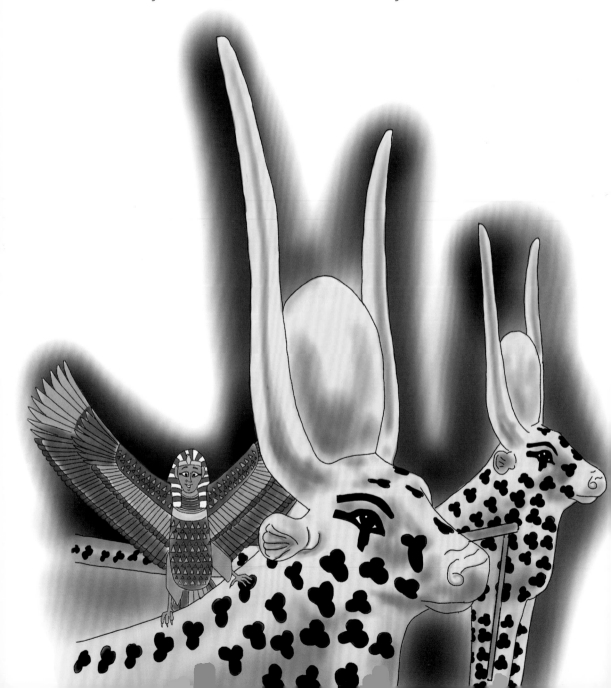

"What are you?" I blurted.

"I'm you," the bird said.

"Me? But I'm here!" I pointed at myself.

"And here. Sort of." The man-bird observed me. "We belong together. I'm your Ba-bird."

"My . . . Ba-bird?"

I remembered being told about Ba-birds. Something to do with our life in the hereafter . . . but I'd been more interested in horses and chariots than in paying much attention. Grandpa Ay had taken care of most of the religious stuff, to keep the priests of the old gods happy after the chaos my father had caused.

"Yes, I told you, we're connected. That's because we're related, in a way," the bird said.

I certainly didn't understand that.

"Here, let me show you." The bird looked toward the two guardian statues.

I opened my mouth to let the bird know that nothing out of the ordinary had happened, when something did: suddenly it was like I was watching through two pairs of eyes. My eyes were looking at the Ba-bird, but at the same time I could see through his eyes, too. I was looking at the guardian statues at the same time! That sure made me feel dizzy.

"Whoaaa . . . !" I stepped back, tripping over the dismantled chariots.

"I am your scout, if you will," the Ba-bird said while I got back to my feet. "I'm here to help you get to the afterlife. Been waiting for you to wake up for a long while. Dozed off myself there."

"How long did I . . . sleep?"

I didn't want to say that I had fainted. Kings don't faint.

"Long enough for them to bury you here and fill your tomb with all this stuff."

The Ba-bird extended a wing in a gesture to take in the whole tomb.

"Bury me? But . . . where am I, then?" I turned to look around the room.

"You are here," the Ba-bird said, nodding toward me. "But your body is over there—behind that wall the guardian statues are guarding. You left it when you died."

I walked closer to the guardian statues, and looked up at them.

"Hello," the one on the left said.

"How do you do?" asked the one on the right.

They both bowed politely.

"Eeek! They talk! They're alive!" I stepped back again, but managed to stay on my feet this time.

"Of course they do. They are to guard your tomb. They couldn't do it if they weren't alive, could they?" the Ba-bird asked matter-of-factly, and fluttered to the top of the head of the statue that had spoken first.

There was a certain logic there. I collected my dignity and bowed my head slightly at the statues. "Nice to meet you, I'm sure," I said.

"Likewise," they both answered.

"So you say my mummy is in there? Behind that wall?" I pointed at the wall behind the guards.

"Yes," all three answered.

"And you said something about walking through walls?" I asked the Ba-bird, who was still sitting atop the guard.

"Yes. You can do that now. But it's rather tight in there," the Ba-bird said. "The whole room is filled with your sarcophagus. So don't just scoot through the wall or you'll find yourself stuck inside the shrine or fall over your dead body. Not that you couldn't get unstuck, but it's a somewhat unpleasant feeling being inside solid things. Go slowly so you can stay near the wall."

Well, there wasn't much else to do but try. I approached the wall, stepping over a chest on the floor, and pushed my hand against it. Solid.

"You have to concentrate your thoughts on going through the wall first. Intention first, action second," the Ba-bird said. I peered closely at him, because he suddenly sounded a lot like my old teacher from the kap.

Then I concentrated on wanting to walk through the wall. At my thought, it changed under my hand, feeling soft and spongy. I took a deep breath. . . .

"You don't need to breathe any more," the Ba-bird said. "You're dead."

"Aha, yes, quite. . . ."

I stepped into the wall. It enveloped me, but the feeling wasn't too uncomfortable, as the material gave way. And now I found myself in the burial chamber where the painters had been working previously. The Ba-bird flew through the wall and landed on top of the shrine.

It hadn't lied. The whole room was almost filled with the shrine that held my sarcophagus—and my mummy. I

walked around the shrine and noticed a pair of eyes on one side; they were meant for my dead body, so that it could look out from the sarcophagus. Which would presumably be quite the boring sight; not that the artists hadn't done a good job when they'd painted the walls of the burial chamber, but just imagine staring at the same painting day after day, month after month, year after year. . . .

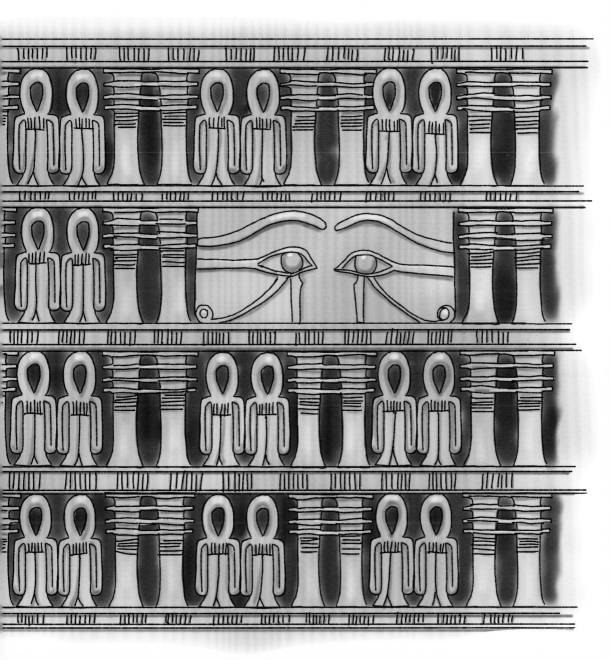

I considered peeking inside the shrine, but the thought of coming face to face with my dead and mummified body didn't feel that attractive. Instead, I just pushed my hand through the shrine wall. There was another wall. And then another. And still one more! Then my fingers touched stone: the sarcophagus. I pushed through that, too, and then my fingers touched what had to be a coffin. I quickly withdrew my hand. I wasn't going to tickle my dead toes.

I heard a cough from behind me. I took another deep breath, which caused the Ba-bird to snort, turned around in the cramped space, and found myself face to face with Anubis.

9 Tomb Robbers

Now, this was a god I knew full well.

"Oh, mighty Anubis!" I fell to my knees. "God of the dead, I greet you!"

"Well, they certainly taught you good manners, but I have to disappoint you somewhat. I am not the god Anubis. I'm a statue made to look like Anubis. And rather a well-made statue at that, if I say so myself."

"Oh. . . ." I got back to my feet, noticing now the carrying poles underneath the gilt pylon he was lying on.

"I'm here to guard you," he said. "I make sure no one gets your innards."

He turned his head to look back, and I noticed a quite beautiful gilded shrine there. A gilded statue of a goddess caught my eye, her hands spread as if hugging the shrine. She had her back to us, but from her headpiece I could tell she was Isis, great in magic. On either side of her I could see two more goddesses, and another behind the shrine.

"Meet Isis, Selket, Nephthys, and Neith," my Ba-bird said. "And the cobras, of course."

I looked at the row of cobras on top of the shrine.

"Erm . . . how do you do?" I said toward the shrine.

"How do you do?" Isis answered.

"How do you do?" three other voices repeated from around the shrine.

"Hissssss," the cobras said, and swayed a little. I supposed that was a greeting.

"Moooo . . . ," came from behind Anubis.

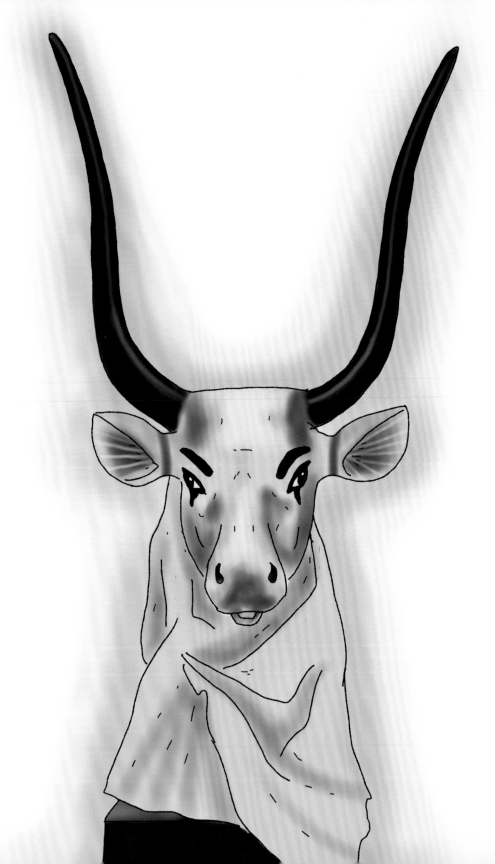

It was a large cow's head. Her skin was golden, her horns were copper, and her eyes were real lapis lazuli.

"Honored to meet you, my lady," I said, bowing respectfully, for surely this was Hathor, who, according to tradition, received the newly dead at the Mountain of the West (which was the mountain above the valley I was buried in). Even though this was another statue, it didn't hurt to be polite, just in case.

"The honor is all mine," the cow said. "I'm pleased to meet such a well-behaved young man."

"Now we need to leave this place and be on our way to the Field of Reeds," the Ba-bird said. "Where's your scroll?"

I didn't understand.

"My scroll? What scroll?"

"Going Forth by Day, of course. Your instructions on how to travel the underworld, get past the dangers there, and arrive at the Fields of Iaru," my Ba-bird said. (I should clarify that he was talking about the Book of the Dead, as you call it these days. And the 'Fields of Iaru' would be what you call 'Heaven.')

"I have no idea about any scrolls. . . ." I looked around me. "They could be anywhere!"

So we began to search. I lifted off the linen cape that Anubis was wearing.

"Hey!" he protested.

"What? Are you cold?"

"No, but it isn't polite to take
someone's clothes off like that!"

"Stop complaining and help us," the Ba-bird
said. "As Tutankhamun here passed out for the
duration of the burial, he didn't see where
everything was put. Try to remember what you saw.
Where could they have put the scroll?"

Anubis got to his feet, shook himself, and jumped down. I
noticed an ivory palette where he had been. I looked closer; it
had been used, and still had green, blue, yellow, red, black, and
white paint on it. There was writing on it, too: 'This belongs to the
royal daughter, Meritaten, beloved and born of the Great Royal Wife

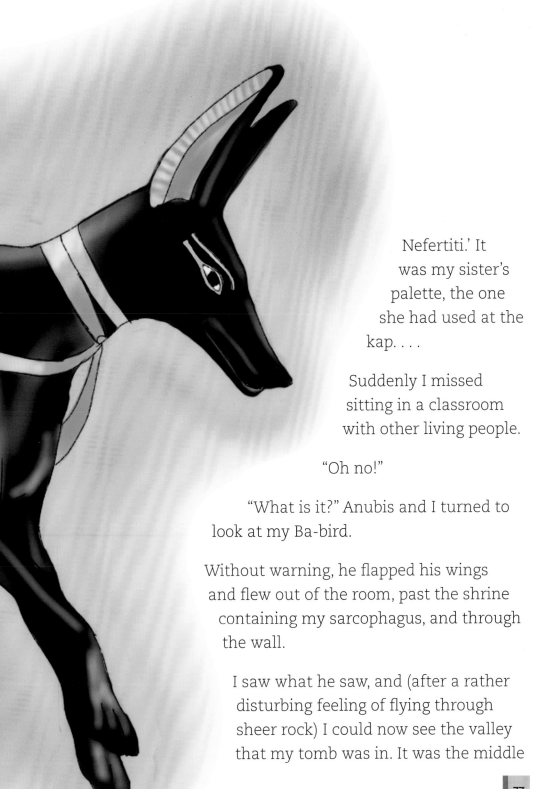

Nefertiti.' It
was my sister's
palette, the one
she had used at the
kap. . . .

Suddenly I missed
sitting in a classroom
with other living people.

"Oh no!"

"What is it?" Anubis and I turned to
look at my Ba-bird.

Without warning, he flapped his wings
and flew out of the room, past the shrine
containing my sarcophagus, and through
the wall.

I saw what he saw, and (after a rather
disturbing feeling of flying through
sheer rock) I could now see the valley
that my tomb was in. It was the middle

of the night, and no one should have been moving there. Yet a group of men were on the steps leading down to my tomb, digging at the wall.

"Thieves!" I shouted. "Thieves are coming!"

The four goddess statues screamed.

"Oh no! Thieves will burn our gilded wood to extract the gold from the ashes!" Selket said, looking at her gilded arms. "And they burn

mummies, too, so the gold in their wrappings melts! They never want anything with your name on it, only melted gold. . . ."

The goddesses let out another scream.

"And they'll steal the jars containing your liver, lungs, intestines, and stomach," Nephthys said. "Not that they want your intestines. They'll throw them away, and keep the jars and sell them! And there you'll be, without your organs! Imagine the afterlife without them!"

Actually, I couldn't imagine that—so far, I felt quite normal and did not know why exactly my mummified organs were necessary in the afterlife. Maybe I'd understand better once I got to the Fields of Iaru.

"And if the thieves can reach your mummy, they'll unwrap you and steal all your amulets and jewelry!" Neith said.

"Or burn you," Selket said.

"Or both!" Nephthys looked very worried.

"Is there nothing we can do?" I asked.

"There might be," Anubis said. "But we have to get to our positions first." Then he yelled, "Boys, are you ready?"

"Yes!" The faint voices of the guardian statues came through the wall.

The goddesses and Anubis went back to their places. We could all now hear the hacking noises, then some rubble falling, and someone coughing.

They had entered my tomb!

I had to see who it was, so I pushed myself through the wall between the guardian statues. Two men were hurriedly opening the caskets and going through them. They seemed to know exactly what they were looking for, and quickly piled jewelry and valuables on pieces of linen that they had laid on the floor. They held oil lamps to help them see. A small opening in the wall revealed another man's face.

"Quickly now! The guards are coming!" the third man hissed.

I looked at my guards; they stood like the wooden statues that they were and said nothing.

"Just a little more! We'll be rich!" the robbers answered. I could see the feverish, greedy look in their eyes. They threw more linen, and sandals, and jewelry, and papyrus scrolls onto the heap.

"Quiet! I hear steps above!" The third man quickly crawled inside the tomb. "Hide the lights! They can't hear or see us if we're quiet and stay in the dark."

Hurriedly the men tied the corners of their bundles, so they could carry the treasure out, and blew the lights out—all but one lamp, which they tried to cover. This was the opportunity my guardians had been waiting for.

I have to say the effect was most satisfactory when the guardian statues stepped forward and the robbers realized that they had moved. For a short moment, they didn't even breathe—and then they took one long breath in and started screaming.

"Ghosts! Demons! The king has come to haunt us!"

They crawled out of the room and vanished. Of course, the racket they had made caught the attention of the valley guards, and we heard yells. My Ba-bird had followed them, so I could see how one of the men was caught. The other two got away with big bundles of valuables.

"Well done, brother!" The guardian statues high-fived each other. "Well done, indeed!" (Yes, we did high-five back then.)

Steps approached. The statues quickly resumed their places, just before a hand pushed an oil lamp into the tomb and a guard of the Valley of the Kings peeked in.

"No one left here, my lord," he said.

Someone crawled in, and much to my surprise I saw my old friend Maya, an official who had been in charge of building my tomb. Not this tomb, though—my intended tomb had not been ready for me when I died.

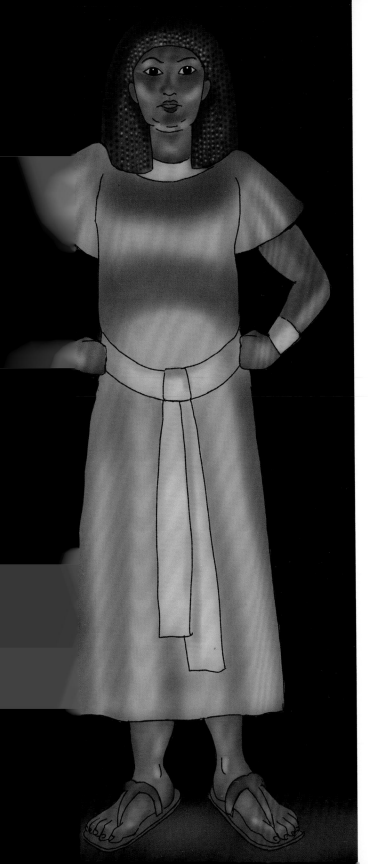

Maya stood up and looked around in the light of the oil lamp that the thieves had left behind.

"Maya!" I shouted at him, but he paid no attention to me.

He gestured to the soldier to follow him. Quickly they cleaned the floor of the things the thieves had thrown around and stuffed them into boxes, looking somewhat scared.

"I should have guessed," Maya said. "The man we caught was one of those who carried these goods into the king's tomb. I'm sure the two that got away are of the same lot. We'll find them all and punish them!"

"Yes, my lord," the soldier said, and looked around, scared.

"We'll go now and the tomb will be resealed," Maya said. "I shall stand guard myself until it's done."

They left the tomb, and after a while men came to rebuild the wall to hide the opening the thieves had made. Even before the sun rose again, the tomb was resealed.

"There's one bad thing that just happened," my Ba-bird said.

"One? They stole my precious jewelry! I'd say that's worth several bad things!" I said.

"Well, one of the thieves took something important from one of the chests here . . . ," my Ba-bird said. "Something more valuable to you than golden trinkets. They took your scroll, Going Forth by Day. Now you can't find your way in the underworld."

"You mean . . . ?"

"I mean, it isn't wise for you to leave this tomb now. Your scroll would have told you exactly what to do and say in the Duat, the underworld. Without it, you'll be a light midnight snack for some hungry demon. And you can't go to the land of the living, either, as you could get mightily lost out there. The winds could carry you to the ends of earth, as you don't really weigh much any more." My Ba-bird sighed. "I hope you find enough here to entertain you for all eternity."

"You mean I'm stuck here? In this little tomb? Forever?"

"Well, unless a miracle happens, yes. With your scroll you could enter the afterlife, but without it I wouldn't try. . . ."

"Midnight snack, you say?"

"Indeed."

The idea of being a walking lunch for demons was not something I wanted to consider. But the thought of staying in my tomb for all eternity was so depressing that I had to sit down on the floor.

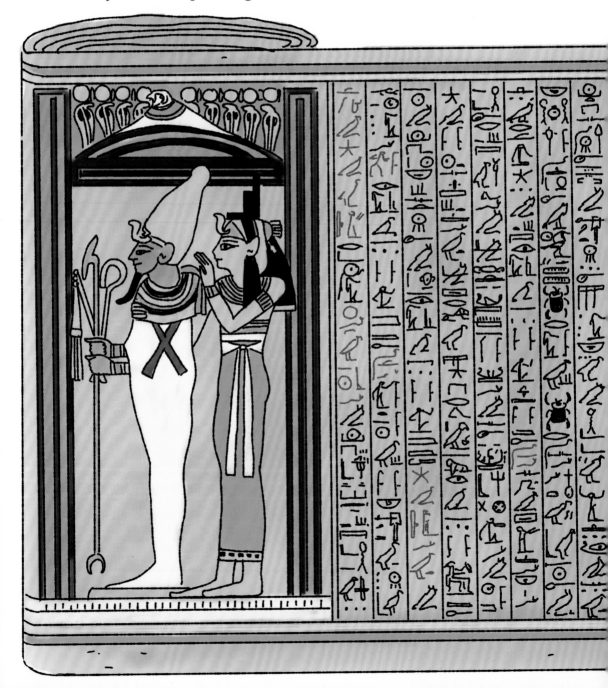

And so began my thousands of years in the tomb. All I could wish for now was a miracle—that someone would bring back my scroll or give me a new one. Otherwise, I would be bored stiff in my tomb, no matter how much company I had.

Luckily, miracles do happen. . . .

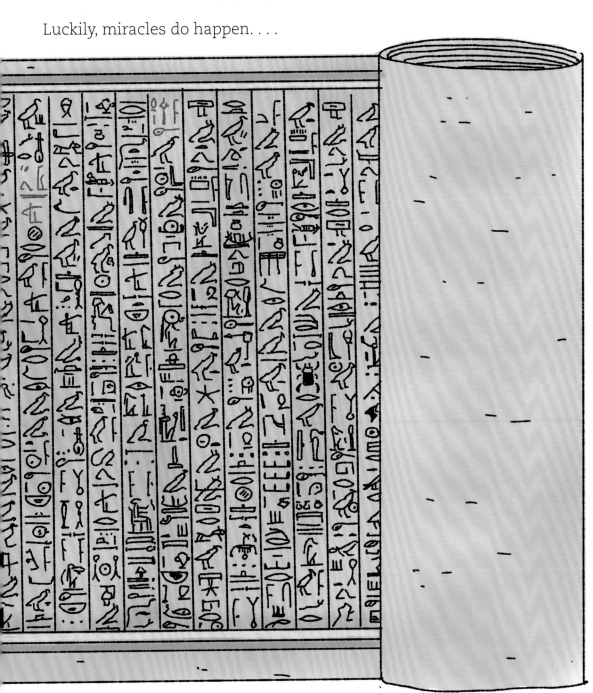

10 Board Games

The miracle didn't happen right away, though.

We had another incident with thieves. It was the two men who had gotten away the first time. This time, they were after my scented oils. The most expensive oils, at that; only royalty could afford perfumed oils. Oils didn't have the king's name written on them and were easy to sell. One of the thieves found some rings they had missed on their first visit and wrapped them in a bundle.

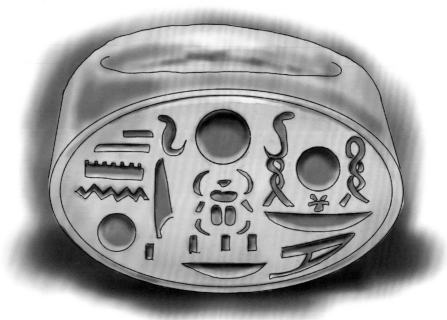

But my trusted friend Maya came to the rescue again. His men caught the thieves as they left the tomb. In the following skirmish, the bundle containing my rings fell to the ground. Again, Maya and his soldiers quickly cleaned up the mess in my tomb, though they didn't notice the rings. I have to say, I was almost happy that the robbers had returned so I could see my old friend again.

Then they resealed the tomb once more, and my Ba-bird showed me how they filled the staircase with stones and rubble until no one could see a single step.

"That should do it," my Ba-bird sighed. "You should be able to keep the rest of your things from now on. Much more comfortable for you, considering you're stuck in here."

I wasn't certain whether I should be happy or not, given that now I'd be alone in my tomb for who knew how long.

Now, I did have company, of course. The goddesses chatted about all sorts of things, but after a while a king gets bored listening to talk about dresses, and wigs, and cosmetics. Even the cobras on top of the shrine where my innards were kept in their canopic jars (and which the goddesses were guarding) tried to get as far from them as they could, so they wouldn't have to listen. (You can't expect snakes to be interested in dresses and such, really.)

I once made the mistake of mentioning this to them, and as a result spent a few years listening to religious talk when they politely changed the subject. They talked about gods, and goddesses, and demons,

and the creation of everything. My head was soon spinning with all the gods who claimed to have created the world, who was married to whom, who was enemy to whom, and so on and so forth. So when the ladies finally returned to talking about dresses, wigs, and cosmetics, I almost sighed with relief.

I had several games in the tomb, and tried playing senet with my shabtis—those would be the little doll-like figurines who were supposed to work for me in the afterlife. What work, you ask? Well, everyone was supposed to work in the afterlife—even kings—but if you had shabtis, they would do your work for you, so you could sit in the gardens and sip juices.

Back to the subject of senet. I tried to play it with Anubis, but as he had no hands, he had to use his teeth to move the pawns. This resulted in damage to the pawns, not to mention the drool . . . yuck! And so I thought I'd put my shabtis to work. I called for them, and they answered, "Here I am!" (That is what their name means.)

Now, the problem was that they all answered when I called, as they didn't have individual names. Since they were also very bored by staying in my tomb for years on end, they started fighting over the right to play with me. I tried not to pay attention to it, but when my whole tomb was full of shabtis shoving each other away from the game (and not being polite about it) and stealing my pawns so they could move them for me (trying to take over the whole game), the day came when I had had enough of picking up the game pieces from the floor. I don't think I managed to finish more than a few games of senet in a hundred years when the shabtis were my opponents.

"Get back to your boxes! Now!" I ordered.

And because they were shabtis, they had to follow my orders. This didn't stop them from grumbling, though, and I could hear their comments through the sides of the boxes they were in:

"Not fair."

"No sense of humor."

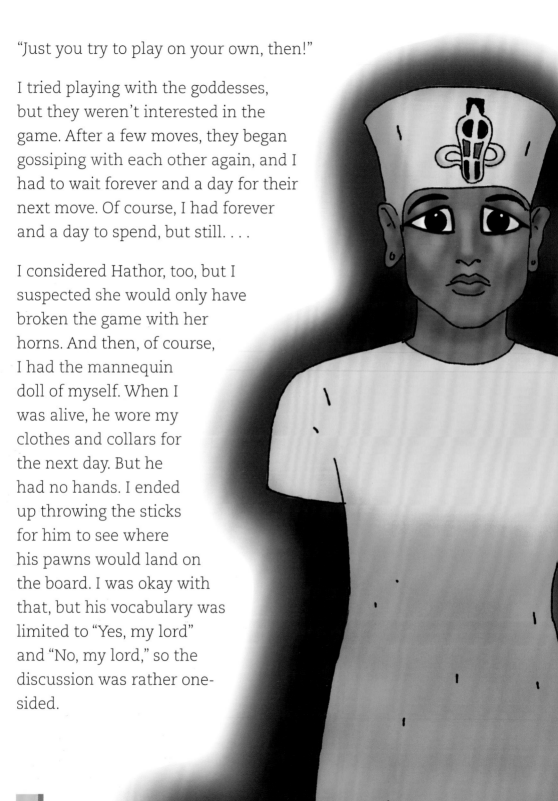

"Just you try to play on your own, then!"

I tried playing with the goddesses, but they weren't interested in the game. After a few moves, they began gossiping with each other again, and I had to wait forever and a day for their next move. Of course, I had forever and a day to spend, but still. . . .

I considered Hathor, too, but I suspected she would only have broken the game with her horns. And then, of course, I had the mannequin doll of myself. When I was alive, he wore my clothes and collars for the next day. But he had no hands. I ended up throwing the sticks for him to see where his pawns would land on the board. I was okay with that, but his vocabulary was limited to "Yes, my lord" and "No, my lord," so the discussion was rather one-sided.

The beds weren't helpful, either; the lion and cow heads had personality problems—it seemed that whoever had put the beds together had named them wrong. Names are very important, after all, as they give you an identity.

The lion-headed bed had been called Mehturt by mistake, which was the name of a celestial cow goddess. And the cow bed had been called Isis-Meht, which was the name of a lioness goddess. Because of this, you just couldn't have a decent conversation with them. The cow bed

tried to roar like a lion . . . and have you ever heard a lion trying to moo?! Quite. There was no way to understand what they were trying to say. And unfortunately they seemed to have lots to say despite their problems with speech. Maybe they understood each other (I have no way of telling), but they certainly seemed to have long, loud conversations that annoyed everyone else. Thankfully there was a lot of linen in my tomb, so the rest of us stuffed our ears with linen balls during especially long conversations.

And the third bed? Well, that was Ammit—a mixture of hippopotamus, leopard, and crocodile. She supposedly represented my rebirth to the afterlife, but she wasn't exactly the happiest of characters. So I didn't even bother asking if she wanted to play senet with me. For all I know, Ammit could have been the monster that ate the hearts of the dead if they hadn't lived good lives. And as any self-respecting Egyptian knows, intelligence and emotions live in the heart. Without your heart, you couldn't reach the afterlife, or so I was told before I died. Anyway, I decided to try to stay on good terms with the Ammit bed—who knew what Ammit might have done after losing a senet game?

My Ba-bird flew out of the tomb every day, so I had a chance to see what was going on in the world outside. (It was like watching TV, as I've later learned.) Without the chance to see the world through my Ba-bird's eyes, I'd have gone gaga in a few years, I'm sure.

Through my Ba-bird's excursions, I learned that Grandpa Ay only ruled for a short while, and then Horemheb took the

crown. The first thing he did was start stealing my monuments for himself. Imagine that, hacking off my name and replacing it with his! It was like he wanted to erase any memory of me. And he did the same to Ay's monuments, and to those of the rest of my family. By the time he died, I was very disappointed in him; I would have spoken my mind, only I couldn't leave my tomb to do so. Eventually, Horemheb slipped into the afterlife, but I still remained stuck in my tomb.

I often cursed the robbers who had stolen my Book of the Dead, but that was no use, as they'd also died long ago and entered the afterlife—using my scroll to guide them, no doubt. . . .

Slowly the years passed, and I witnessed kings coming and going. One day, it rained in the desert and a flash flood hit the valley where my tomb was, and the mud and stones it brought with it hid the entrance to my tomb completely. Later, workers building another royal tomb built their huts right above the entrance of mine without ever knowing it was there!

Then things went wrong in the kingdom of Egypt, and through the eyes of my Ba-bird I witnessed several tomb robberies of the worst kind. And one day, priests came and collected the remaining mummies of the kings whose tombs had been robbed, and placed them all in one tomb. I felt sorry for all the kings who no longer had any treasures left.

When my Ba-bird flew greater distances, I saw a great city being built on the shore of the Great Green (the Mediterranean Sea, as you call it). It was called Alexandria. A great lighthouse shone its light over the sea, guiding ships to the harbor. A most ingenious invention!

And then, one day, there were no more Egyptian rulers. The last one, Cleopatra the Seventh, died, and the Romans took over.

It was sad to see how old Egypt was forgotten when no one could read our writings any more. People showed no respect to old buildings, and tore them down to use the stone in their own houses. Great armies marched over the land.

Finally, one day, people became interested in us again! They found a stone that helped them to learn to read our ancient writings again. (It's called the Rosetta Stone, and you can see it at the British Museum.) I learned that the scientist who finally 'cracked the code,' as you would say, was called Champollion. Now people found Egypt even more fascinating.

This interest caused a lot of digging to occur throughout the land, especially in the Valley of the Kings. Through the eyes and ears of my Ba-bird, I slowly learned to understand the languages that these diggers used. Learning new languages eased my boredom a lot.

Then, at last, my Ba-bird showed me that they were digging away the rubble that had covered the stairs to my tomb for so long. I waited eagerly by the wall as they made a hole in it. I would see living people again! Anubis took his place on top of his pylon, shabtis scurried to their boxes (I no longer forced them to stay there all the time), and the goddesses ran to protect my innards again. I was a bit ashamed that we hadn't kept the tomb clean; things were lying around everywhere.

A hand pushed through the hole they had made, holding a candle. The light flickered, reflecting from the gilded beds.

"Well, can you see anything?" a man's voice asked.

"Yes. Wonderful things!" was the answer.

And that's how my tomb was found on 26 November 1922. The man holding the candle was called Howard Carter, and he spent the next few years in my tomb. But he didn't come to steal—oh no, he came to save all my belongings so they wouldn't be destroyed.

11 Getting Out

It took Mr. Carter and his team years to go through all the things in my tomb. I spent much of that time by his shoulder, watching with interest everything he did. There was a Mr. Burton, too, who had a strange gadget that he pointed at all my treasures before they were carried away. I understood that it somehow painted a picture of each object for later viewing. I never saw any of these paintings, though, until several years later. You call these magical paintings 'photographs.' It really is great magic—the painter must have been tiny, or invisible, or both.

After Mr. Burton's magical box had painted a picture of each of my possessions, they were carried out one by one. Strangely, they didn't just step into the room and take my treasures away like the tomb robbers had. For some reason, they started with the closest things and slowly moved their way into the tomb. They waited for four years before they got into the room where Anubis was waiting to be carried out.

I quite admired their patience—it had something to do with what they called their 'scientific approach.'

"Do I still need to stay here?" I asked my Ba-bird. "I mean, after everything's been carried away? In an empty tomb?"

"The winds may still take you if you leave," he told me. "But if someone would agree to come here from the Fields of Iaru and accompany you, they could keep you from flying off with the winds."

"Could we send word to the afterlife? To someone I knew?"

"We could try . . . ," my Ba-bird mused. "I'd need to find a tomb with a door to the afterlife first, though. You never had a proper door to the afterlife in your tomb. If you'd had one, your family and friends could have come to keep you company. Maybe they could even have helped you to reach the Fields of Iaru."

"A door?"

"Yes, a door to the afterlife. Our kind walk through what these new people would call 'false doors' to reach the land of the living. We can't just walk through the walls to and from the afterlife. But once a dead person has entered the land of the living through such a door, they can move about there. Now that the door to your tomb is open, someone might well enter. Yes, that's a good idea! I'll go and find a 'false door,' and ask if anyone would be willing to come to you."

He flew off. I stared around the small rooms of my tomb, worried at how bored I'd be with nothing to entertain myself. I even missed the chatter of the goddesses and the shabtis.

My Ba-bird flew around for a while, and then he showed me a tomb he had flown into. I had no idea whose tomb it was, but there was a stylized door built into it. The doorway was too narrow for any living person to walk through.

My Ba-bird did or said something, because suddenly light shone through the false door as if someone had opened it from the other side . . . and then a figure came through. It was like this figure slid sideways through the narrow opening like a piece of papyrus. My Ba-bird had connected with someone in the afterlife! My connection through the Ba-bird's eyes was lost at this point, so I had to wait until he returned to see who it was he'd brought back with him. Maybe it was Grandpa Ay? Or maybe Horemheb? Or Ankhesenamun?

"Look who came to accompany you out of your tomb!"

My Ba-bird flew back inside, and behind him came a small mummified figure. It was Fingers!

He looked around, interested in all the goings-on. The moment he saw me, he gave a happy shriek and ran to me, climbing up my leg and settling on my

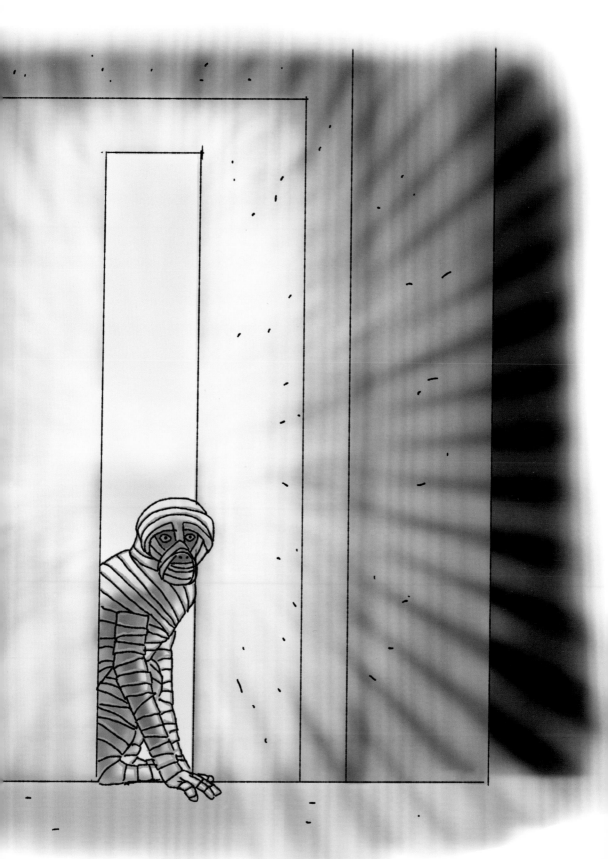

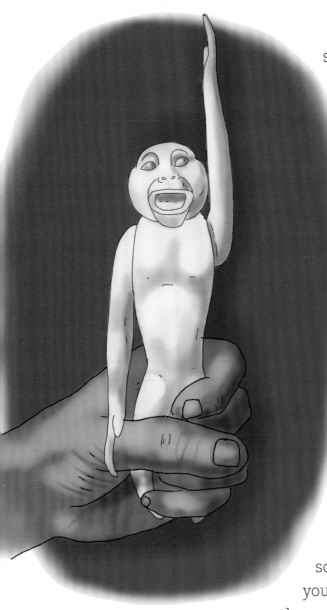

shoulder, and hugged my head. I was so happy to see him. After his death, I hadn't wanted another monkey, but had only had toy monkeys—it hurt too much to lose him, and I didn't want to experience that again.

"But . . . how can Fingers keep me from flying away into the sky when I leave the tomb?" I asked. "He's so small!"

"He's been properly mummified and buried, and after that he can enter the world of the living quite normally and can't be whisked off by winds. He's solid enough. You need to attach yourself to him somehow, and then you should be safe. His small size doesn't matter—he'll keep you grounded."

I looked around. What could I use to attach Fingers to me? He seemed very happy to be on my shoulder at present, but he was a monkey, and monkeys tend to jump off when the mood takes them.

Thankfully, he had been well mummified, and I was glad I had ordered that the finest long linen strips be used to do this. I took the end of one strip that Fingers offered to me, and with a little effort I managed to free a long enough section to tie around my wrist. Fingers didn't seem to mind.

"Well, then. I suppose now there's nothing left but to walk out of the tomb!" my Ba-bird said.

I took a deep breath.

"You don't need to do that, you're already dead," my Ba-bird said out of habit.

And then I just walked out of my tomb, past the workers and into the sunlight. Fingers ran beside me.

Oh, the joy of seeing the sun again! I spread my arms, breathed in deeply. . . .

"You don't need—" my Ba-bird began.

Which is when the wind took me. I flew up into the sky— and then the strip of linen tied to Fingers stopped me. I looked down, and Fingers looked up. He gave an amused scream. I grasped the linen strip and pulled my way back down. Thankfully, it held, and I didn't unwrap Fingers, either. I was like what you call a balloon. Weightless, bobbing in the wind.

"Where to now?" I asked my Ba-bird.

"I suggest we go where your tomb goods have been taken," my Ba-bird said, and flew toward another tomb.

"They've carried my goods to another tomb? Whatever for?"

"To repair them and prepare them for a long journey."

"A journey where?"

"To a museum."

"What's that?"

"A place where old things are displayed so that anyone can come and see them."

A thought came to me. "All sorts of old things?"

"Yes, every imaginable type of thing."

"Like . . . old writings?"

"Yes. . . ."

"Like . . . there might be a Book of the Dead, too?"

"Good thinking!" my Ba-bird admitted. "There just may be a spare scroll for you there."

My Ba-bird showed the way, and we followed. We managed to get to the tomb where my things were with only two detours—a pretty good achievement for a monkey! First, Fingers jumped onto the shoulder of a lady who was eating a fruit I later learned to be an apple. He tried to grab the fruit, but couldn't. The lady munched away until she'd eaten the whole thing, and no matter how much

Fingers tried to grasp the fruit, his hands couldn't get hold of it. The resulting annoyance caused Fingers to jump up and down on the lady's headpiece (a most strange looking thing).

But she paid no attention to the monkey, and after a while Fingers climbed down. Then he saw another little monkey on the shoulder of a man in a long robe who seemed to be selling water, and ran over to meet it.

The animal was able to see Fingers, which was quite interesting. It jumped down from its owner's shoulder while he sold water to thirsty passersby. They chatted monkey talk together for a while, but then the man turned to walk away toward a new group of people, and the monkey had to follow him.

It was good to see my belongings again, and Fingers also enjoyed climbing on them. The guardian statues took a liking to him, and he sat for long hours on their shoulders. I was quite impatient, waiting for the day when all the goods would be taken to the museum and I could go and see if they had a scroll that I could use to enter the afterlife.

But a strange thing happened: the more time I spent with Fingers, the more solid I seemed to become. I was no longer whisked off by wind as long as Fingers was near me. Soon, I no longer needed to be tied to him. My Ba-bird explained that it had to do with Fingers having made a promise to be my guide. If Fingers went away, I became lighter and lighter, so I tried to keep him amused so he'd stay near me.

Finally, one day, everything was packed and carried to boxes that moved in a strange way: there were metal pieces called 'rails,' and the boxes had little wheels underneath that moved on them. When the boxes reached the end of the rails, they were lifted up and carried to the front of the boxes, and the whole process started again.

It was slow going, but I didn't mind. It was most interesting to see this new way of moving things. In my time, sledges were used. Water (or milk, on special occasions) was poured on the ground in front of the sledge so it would move more easily. The thought of using metal bars to create a road for the sledge had never occurred to anyone in my time—probably because there would never have been enough metal.

It took hours and hours to get the boxes to the river. I sat on top of them, admiring the scenery. I saw the great river again after 3,300 years. I breathed in and out, accompanied by the 'no need' comments of my Ba-bird, and could not have been happier.

And how did it feel to be able to travel in a ship downriver again? Wonderful! Though I have to say, I was surprised at the things I saw—so much had changed during my absence!

And then we came to where my old capital, Inbu-Hedj (Memphis), had been. A sprawling city with magnificent buildings was there now. I stared at the pyramids, which looked strange; the white stones that had once covered them had all been stripped off. It seemed that the old habit of reusing building materials was alive and well. But that had always been the way of things. . . .

Fingers wanted to go and explore the city immediately, but somehow my Ba-bird managed to persuade him to come to the museum instead.

I was glad of this, for I felt right at home at the Egyptian Museum in Cairo.

Traveling the World

And did I find a scroll, a Book of the Dead of my own?

There were so many things in the museum that I spent many months just looking at everything and talking to all the objects who could answer back. No living being seemed to hear their voices, but being dead has its advantages. I learned a lot about the history of ancient Egypt through these discussions.

I also learned that there were still tomb robbers about. Many objects had been taken from these thieves and

brought to the museum, and the archaeologists and Egyptologists were sad to see them—well, they were happy to see the stolen items in a museum, but unhappy because they didn't know where they'd been stolen from. They wished they could have seen the things in their original tombs, so they could have learned more about life in ancient Kemet. Old things should be left where they're found so your scientists can learn from them and then take proper care of them, to make sure they aren't destroyed.

So, there I was at the museum. As it happened, there were so many things, including scrolls and writings, in the museum storage that one day I came across the very thing I was looking for: a Book of the Dead. And did I take it? Yes, I did. Now, you may call this stealing, but as the scroll's original owner was nowhere to be seen and my own scroll had been stolen. . . .

I made a promise, though, that in return for the scroll, after I had reached the afterlife and could move about in the land of the living without the help of Fingers, I would go around the country in search of other dead people who had been stuck in their tombs, and offer the scroll for their use.

However, I did not leave immediately for the afterlife after finding this scroll. The museum was too interesting a place. And then, when I thought the time had come for me to finally leave, I heard that some of my possessions were going on a tour around the world. How could I resist going with them? Ah, to see the modern world! I decided to stay a bit longer to be able to do that.

And so I have traveled with my treasures to the United States, Japan, France, the Soviet Union, Canada, England, and West Germany—countries I had never even heard of, as they came into existence thousands of years after my life. Fingers has been with me all the time. He also seems to enjoy seeing new places. And he still tries to steal fruit wherever we are; his lack of success hasn't discouraged him in the least.

It has been most heartwarming to see how interested people are in my life and death; even to a degree where my actual possessions were not enough, and replicas were made of them so that more people could see my treasures. And very good replicas they were, too!

I was somewhat shocked to learn what had happened to my body, though. Can you believe that they used such unguents and oils in my mummification that I actually caught fire in the coffin? Yes, you heard me right. The embalmers should have known better, for goodness' sakes. But, for some reason, they'd poured bucketfuls of oils and flammable materials over me, and poof! Not long after my burial, I was on fire! And there I was in the tomb and never knew this had happened. The fire never spread outside my coffin, thankfully, but it did leave my body in a somewhat toasty condition.

And when they finally got me loose from my wrappings, my head had fallen off! Oh yes, I was a headless person. And on top of that, I was a heartless king, too! I had no heart left, and was missing ribs and all sorts of things that are necessary if you intend to continue living. So what exactly happened that I ended up in a coffin without a heart and ribs? I've tried to figure this out myself. But my last memory is of racing my chariot, and that's all.

I'm leaning toward the theory that I fell off my chariot, and when I got up and was still on my knees, another chariot drove over me and crushed me. Some researchers who specialize in accidents caused by your horseless carriages have come to this conclusion, anyway. But, as I said, I don't remember a thing, so I can't be sure. First, I was alive, and then I was standing inside my tomb, quite dead.

Oh, one more thing before I finish. I've learned that people think there was a curse on my tomb: that anyone entering my tomb would die a horrible death, or something of the sort. Well, no, there's no such thing as a curse. It's true that the gentleman who made it possible for Mr. Carter to examine my tomb and take such good care of the objects there died of an infected mosquito bite. Lord Carnarvon, he was called. . . . But that was no curse. I'm no mosquito, and I certainly didn't bite him; it was an insect that no ancient Egyptian ever liked. They also say that this electric light you've invented failed at the moment of his death; but as far as I've heard, the electricity in Cairo wasn't exactly reliable at the time when my tomb was discovered. So, a coincidence, I'd say. The lights went out all the time. . . . And they still do.

I learned that supposedly there had been a curse written over the doorway of my tomb, promising swift death to anyone who entered. Right. Had that been true—and had any such curse actually worked—isn't it interesting that Mr. Carter spent ten whole years inside the tomb and then continued his life quite normally after that? The curse is nonsense, pure nonsense. The only curse I know about is me saying a few choice words about those tomb robbers stealing my Book of the Dead.

Lord Carnarvon's dog Susie, you ask? The one who died England, supposedly at the exact time when Lord Carnarvon died in Egypt? No curse there, either. Lord Carnarvon died at around 2 a.m. in Cairo, which would have been midnight in England. And Susie the dog died at 4 a.m. English time. Yes, I've done my research. A coincidence again, I say. But I'm sure Lord Carnarvon was happy to see his dog in the afterlife, just as I was happy to meet Fingers again.

All in all, being dead isn't all that bad. I don't get tired, and can travel the world and see people and places. It's fun to put my head inside my golden mask and look through its eyes at the tourists oohing and aah-ing in front of it. Sometimes I'm almost certain that some people see me there, for they suddenly lean forward and look into the mask's eyes. Children, especially, seem to spot me there. I, of course, wave at them and try to say hello, but most people don't hear me. Maybe no one does. But again, I have a feeling that some children do. . . .

It's been fun, but I think I'll soon take my scroll and head for the afterlife. I've heard that Ankhesenamun, my parents, my sisters, and many people I knew have been asking when I'll come home, so I suppose I'd better go and greet them soon. They have been waiting to see me for a long time already. But I'll be back again. There are many false doors in museums which I can use to return. So if you ever stand in a museum in front of my golden mask, have a look into its eyes and you may just see me there!

Until we meet again, in the ancient Egyptian manner, I wish you life, prosperity, and health!

TUTANKHAMUN